THE CAT WHO TASTED CINNAMON TOAST

THE CAT WHO TASTED

CINNAMON TOAST,

 *by Ann Spencer*   *Alfred A. Knopf, New York   1968*

This is a Borzoi Book
Published by Alfred A. Knopf, Inc.
First Edition
Copyright © 1968 by Ann Spencer
All rights reserved under International and Pan-American
Copyright Conventions. Distributed by Random House, Inc.
Published simultaneously in Toronto, Canada, by Random House of Canada Limited.
Library of Congress Catalog Card Number: 68-13644
Manufactured in the United States of America

THE CAT WHO TASTED CINNAMON TOAST

iss Margrove was drinking her tea one day . . .

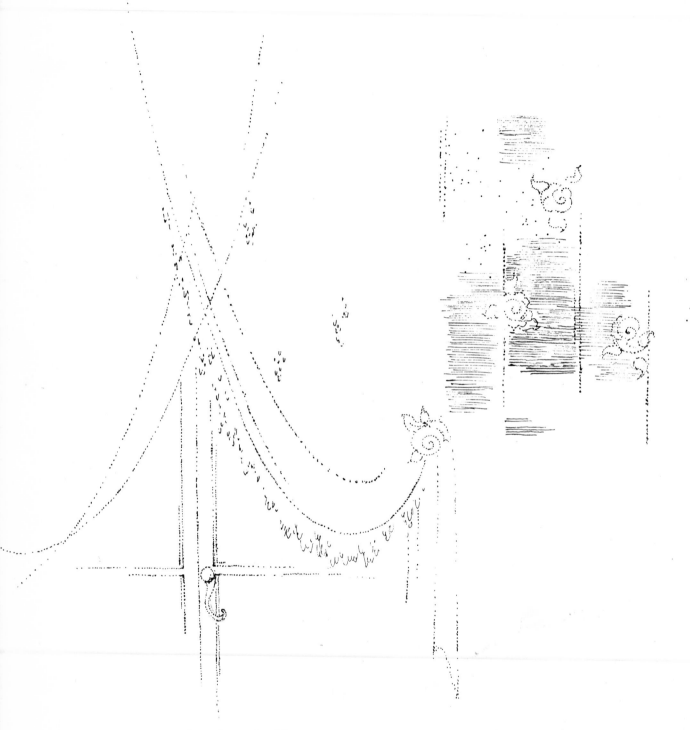

when she noticed her cat,

Augie, looking at her in a funny way.

His platter of fresh filet of horsemeat lay untouched. Miss Margrove sniffed it, stuck out a tentative finger, tasted it. It passed the test, but Augie would have none of it. So she sighed and bit into a piece of cinnamon toast. Augie continued to stare until she broke off a little piece and handed it down to him.

He scooped

it up

in both paws . . .

stuffed it into his mouth and gulped.
Then he settled back on his haunches
and ogled Miss Margrove some more.
She finally surrendered the whole
piece of toast and he pounced
on it with a growl of victory.

Poor little Augie, thought Miss Margrove.

He has a sweet tooth just like everybody else.

And she picked him up and hugged him.

The next day Augie skipped his breakfast. Instead he squatted down on the sideboard and watched Miss Margrove eat her kippers. Each morsel, as it traveled from the plate to Miss Margrove's mouth, was followed by Augie's large yellow eyes. He waved a supplicating paw in the air, and Miss Margrove gave him the rest of her kippers.

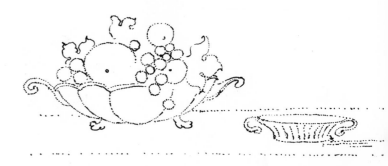

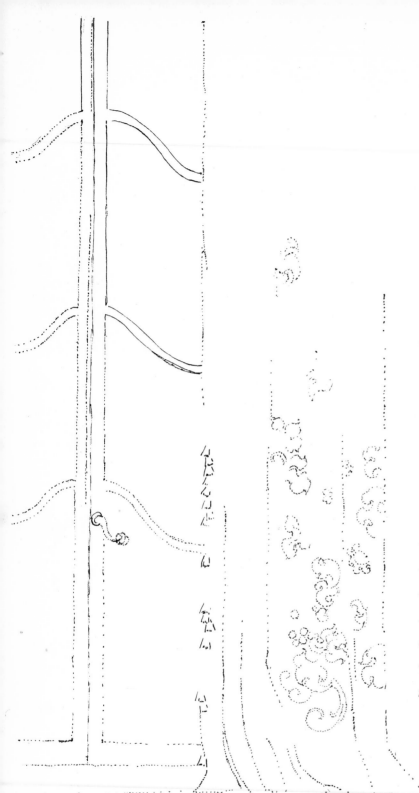

Augie slept through lunch,
somewhat to Miss Margrove's relief.
She feared that if he wheedled
too many indigestible tidbits
out of her he might come down with
some fearful nutritional disease.
Cat pellagra, maybe. Was there
such a thing? She'd heard that white
bread sometimes drove them mad.
At dinner as a precautionary measure,
she sent him into the kitchen.
But Augie hid behind the pantry
door and when the soup course
was wheeled in he crept in
under the serving table . . .

leaped onto the sideboard,
and turned his yellow gimlet
eyes on Miss Margrove's duck
à l'orange. She meekly delivered
over the breast to him while
she nibbled on a wing.

The next day . . .
he had Canadian bacon
for breakfast . . .

for lunch he scooped all the clams out of the chowder ...

for tea he wolfed down all the petits fours . . .

and for dinner finished off all the
hors d'oeuvres and Miss Margrove's
truite amandine, leaving her
only the fish heads.

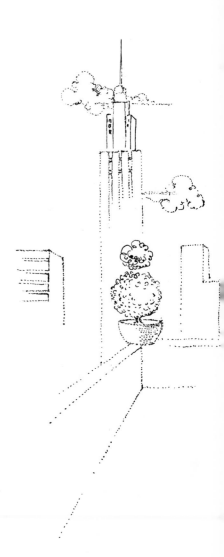

The following morning Miss Margrove telephoned Augie's veterinarian, Dr. Orval Dropsey, and described Augie's symptoms. Dr. Dropsey privately concluded that Augie was merely spoiled, but all he said to Miss Margrove was "Holy Moses" or some other mild expletive he reserved for his silver-haired clientele. He suggested starving Augie into submission. A day or two of fasting ought to get his mind off haute cuisine and back where it belonged, on Texas horsemeat. So for two days while Augie's awful cries of hunger echoed up the dumb-waiter from the servants' quarters below, Miss Margrove steeled herself and knitted. On the third day an attractive platter of horsemeat tenderloin garnished with parsley was presented to the famished Augie. Deceived by its appearance, he thought it was chateaubriand, but the gamy odor of horse was a giveaway, and in a fury he hauled the platter out onto the roof and flung it at the neighbor's pet vulture, who received this sudden gift from heaven with a grateful caw.

Miss Margrove capitulated and gave Augie a large serving of buttered asparagus. He ate it down to the last stalk and licked the plate so clean that some of the gold enamel started to come off. Miss Margrove grew increasingly alarmed. Either her Augie must be the reincarnation of Lucullus or he had been born too soon in the history of cat evolution: from fastidious gourmet he might suddenly turn boulevardier and stride off on his two hind paws with her Greatuncle Alex's gold-headed cane.

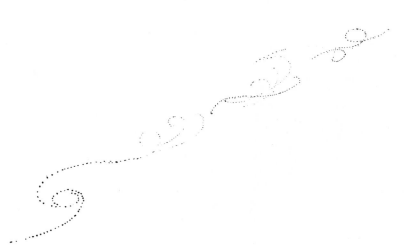

*As she pondered this question a Bell Telephone commercial was blaring on her TV set.
"Let your fingers do the walking. Use the Yellow Pages," it suggested.
And the power of suggestion led her to the directory where
she found just what she was looking for under
PSYCHIATRY: Cats. She called the
number and made an appointment.*

So Augie was bundled up in his purple afghan

and rolled off in the Rolls . . .

to see Dr. Fogg: Psychiatrist to Cats, domestic.

When the doctor saw Augie he

took off his rimless distance glasses,

put on his tortoiseshell reading

glasses, and gazed eyeball to eyeball

into Augie's superb yellow orbs . . .

*Unfortunately he had just
been nibbling absent-mindedly on
oyster crackers, a plebeian note
that was highly offensive to
Augie. So he hauled off . . .*

and swiped Dr. Fogg on the nose.

*R*ubbing his injured member ruefully, he pronounced Augie a "somewhat unusual cat" and then asked a few pointed questions about inbreeding. But since all Augie's forebears were healthily melting-pot (it was rumored that he had been born in a bowling alley in Secaucus, New Jersey), the question remained unanswered. When, as Miss Margrove dreaded, he finally broached the subject of toilet training, she stammered something about a roof garden full of tubs of humus where tall cypress grew. The doctor finally decided that Augie's major personality change had been brought on by five monotonous years of rigidly supervised diet and recommended a complete change of scene. So Augie and Miss Margrove set off in the Rolls for Sea Island, Georgia.

*But in Georgia the smell
of iodine in the sea air went to Augie's
head and he got hooked on caviar.*

*At twenty dollars an ounce
this was a little too much for even Miss
Margrove's millions, so they hastened
back to the relative austerity
of penthouse living.*

*Things went along fairly
well for a while, with Miss Margrove
and Augie dining deux à deux, meal after meal.
A certain rhythm took over at meal hours.
It was "one for you" and "one for me"
as they shared the oysters Rockefeller.*

This not unhappy détente could have gone on indefinitely but for a fatal error. Miss Margrove gave a Chinese luncheon for the Bryn Mawr class of 1910 . . .

Augie made the rounds . . .
From then on he would eat nothing but mandarin duck.
The French chef left in a huff.

To appease his Oriental mood, proud Miss Margrove had to lure the cook away from the Chinese consul who lived across the street. But no sooner had he unpacked his chopsticks than Augie crawled down the fire escape and had a culinary adventure in a restaurant called the Omar Khayyam . . .

where an unknown benefactor staked him to a free lunch.

After this exotic experience his demands knew no bounds. While newspaper headlines announced the latest flight around the globe of a new space hero, Augie had quietly

set out on a culinary armchair tour of his own.

As the spaceship drifted over Tokyo

he savored sukiyaki.

*He nibbled on shish kebab as
it floated by the Gulf of Aden,*

and drank an apéritif

as it passed over Paris.

A whole flotilla of chefs had to be hired, and soon the whole household echoed with the clatter from the kitchen and the bickering in many tongues.

Miss Margrove suddenly felt superfluous. A visit to the Philadelphia branch of the Margroves seemed in order, and she set off for Chestnut Hill.

*N*ow Augie settled down to la vie en rose in earnest. There were occasional thorns —like the Christmas turkey that was still being served up as croquettes until Augie flung the carcass over the parapet to his old friend the vulture. He never quite understood spaghetti. Somehow he got it all confused with Miss Margrove's knitting. The subtle mystery of artichokes eluded him entirely . . .

and once he got drunk on baba au rhum.

But he had the world by the tail again when his lady of the moment came to dinner. Unfortunately she was a puss from the hintervald reared only on kitty food, and she passed out over her first dish of escargots in garlic sauce.

He revived her with ice cream
and quickly initiated her into all the new flavors:
Hawaiian punch and pineapple, cocoanut and
passion fruit. She was mad for pink grapefruit,
and Augie's favorite was licorice, which he
consumed with relish on a Queen Anne chair.

*About this time a crisis was brewing
in the kitchen. Surfeited with so many delicacies,
Augie's appetite grew jaded, and the chefs despaired
of awakening it. Often now he would snooze through
a meal, giving way to involuntary twitches as memories
of Miss Margrove crept into his subconscious.
Finally the chefs all shouldered their
casseroles and departed . . .*

. . . and Miss Margrove returned home.

*W*hen he saw his mistress, Augie rolled out of an ancestral
armchair and with a noisy chirrup padded happily over to greet her.
He ran excitedly in and out of the kitchen, but Miss Margrove could only
stumble after him, distraught to find that all the chefs were gone. Who would
feed Augie now? Who would provide him with all the fine gourmet fare
his sensitive tastebuds craved? Who . . . but Miss Margrove,
Miss Margrove who had scarcely set foot in a kitchen.

*Suddenly a voice from beyond
seemed to summon her.*

"Welcome to 'The French Chef'!"
it said.

Miss Margrove stood at attention
watching this comforting woman cradle a
huge fish. "There is no trick at all to cooking
a ten-pound salmon," the voice went on.
"All it does is sit quietly in liquid."

In the refrigerator lay a long, limp, speckled creature
with a glassy eye, which by some happy chance
the smörgasbord chef must have left behind,
and Miss Margrove went into action. When her
instructress suggested a jumbo wash boiler
would do for a fish boiler, Miss Margrove
produced a family heirloom.

Lacking the suggested layers of cheesecloth,
she seized upon one of her hairnets to serve
as a sling and gingerly lowered
the fish into its bath.

Exhausted by her efforts, Miss Margrove dozed off. When she awoke there was much spluttering at the stove and the quiet bath in which her salmon should have been resting had turned into a seething caldron. Miss Margrove jabbed a fork into the brew and a fleshless head followed by thirty inches of skeleton greeted her sad gaze.

Using a sieve, she did manage to retrieve
a few pieces of salmon and dump them
onto a waiting platter.

Augie sniffed at them gingerly,
scooped up a morsel with his
paw, and nibbled on it reflectively.

Then he ate it all up

and asked for more.

Somewhere at the bottom of his hedonish
little soul was a spark of grace. He felt
sorry for Miss Margrove.

Strenuous days followed, as Augie's mistress struggled with curdled hollandaise, lumpy cheese fondues, and the decline and fall of all her soufflés. At length the time came when a soufflé held its ground and the tide of battle turned. Then before you could say "Escoffier" she was whipping up béchamel sauce with one hand while she turned the fish with the other.

From then on she went on from triumph to triumph and Augie lived la vie en rose again. Sometimes just for variety he and Miss Margrove ate out. They were often seen at the Tavern on the Green nibbling on cucumber sandwiches. They were regular habitués at the Pavillon, which employed Miss Margrove's former French chef, who now smiled forgiveness at Augie.

*A*nd on rare days in June . . .

they had picnics on the beach at Southampton.

As they drifted quietly into old age together
Augie slowed down a little. He was often quite content
with a modest little spinach soufflé or a bowl of
onion soup. And in the evenings they both snoozed
peacefully together in the big ancestral armchair
while visions of banquets past . . .

floated peacefully through their dreams.

A Note About the Author

*Ann Spencer was born in 1918 in New Hope, Pennsylvania,
and is the daughter of the well-known impressionist painter
Robert Spencer and Margaret Spencer, one of America's first
woman architects. She lived in Paris as a girl but returned to the
United States in her late teens to study at the Art Students League
in New York City. Miss Spencer's artistic talents range from the
delightful line drawings with which she has illustrated this book,
through lithographs, to satirical paintings that are in many
collections throughout the Southwest. Ann Spencer is married
to Lewis R. Simon and lives in Tucson, Arizona,
with her husband and the prototype of Augie.*

A Note on the Type

*The text of this book has been set on the Monotype in
"Fournier," a type face so called after James Simon Fournier,
a celebrated type designer in eighteenth-century France. Fournier's
type is considered transitional in that it drew its inspiration
from the old style, yet was ingeniously innovational,
providing for an elegant yet legible appearance.*

*After his death in 1768, Fournier was
remembered primarily as the author of a famous
manual of typography and as a pioneer of the point
system until 1925, when the Monotype Corporation
of London revived Fournier's roman and italic.
The composition was done by the Press of A. Colish,
Mt. Vernon, N.Y., printed by the Halliday
Lithograph Corp., West Hanover, Mass., and bound
by Economy Bookbinding Corp., Kearny, N.J.*